FIVE HOURS

CRAIG R. BAXLEY

Visit Craig R. Baxley at www.CraigBaxley.com
Or write author@CraigBaxley.com

Formatting, Editing, and Cover Design by Michele Pollock Dalton of Barr26 Creative Services | www.Barr26CreativeServices.com

Printed in the United States of America

Paperback ISBN: 979-8-9851952-7-9
eBook ISBN: 979-8-9851952-8-6

For Valerie

CONTENTS

PROLOGUE

Living clouds drifted across an arid plain, painted like a Thomas Moran portrait that captured the mind-blowing landscape. Locust made a steady, unnerving sound while an orange ball was slowly swallowed by the horizon.

Golden grass rippled as the wind slowly snaked through it. And an otherworldly light seeped away across the vast expanse of the Zuni Pueblo Reservation in Grants County, one hundred fifty miles south of Black Rock, New Mexico.

The breeze swelled, whistling and moaning, as an American flag flapped above an ancient Airstream trailer – its busted screen door creaking in the wind.

Somewhere a dog barked as a rhythmic rumble slowly began to grow louder.

A sharp gust snapped a sheet of plastic in the window. Inside, a lamp illuminated a silhouette that stood motionless.

A pair of black eyes watched. An ancient hand ran over the top of a cigarette pack, like a blind man reading Braille.

Outside, a pick-up rumbled into view amid swirling dust and pelting sand. It rolled to an abrupt stop.

That morning, he had raced across the flatlands of New Mexico.

Polarized aviator sunglasses shielded the driver's eyes from the sun. He climbed out, his eyes fixed on the silhouette in the window. Then he reached inside the pick-up and pulled out a briefcase.

As he moved away from the vehicle with the briefcase in hand, a diamondback rattler coiled, rattling and hissing. With starling quickness, the visitor pulled a Glock-19 and fired once.

The gunshot echoed through the valley, booming like the aftermath of dynamite.

With a final blinding display, the flaming sun extinguished itself on the horizon.

CHAPTER 1

A white band cracked the pre-dawn horizon of the barren Mexican desert. The sun had barely begun to appear.

Somewhere on Route 81 in the Chihuahua Desert, a dark shape continued to grow through a collage of shimmering heat waves, slowly evolving into a black 707-hp Jeep Grand Cherokee Trackhawk.

Inside it was silent, except for the steady hum of the supercharged Hellcat V8 under the hood.

The driver, Jack Mathews, was in his mid-thirties - lean with dark hair and discerning, intelligent eyes. He looked up at his reflection in the rearview, then back at the road. He wore a dark t-shirt and faded jeans.

He glanced over at his passenger, Samantha Collins, and asked, "Did I do anything last night I should know about?"

Sam had long brown hair and was slim and attractive - sunglasses hid her blue eyes. Her eyes refocused and blinked to attention.

"You okay, Sam?" he asked.

She brushed her hair back and looked over at him. "I couldn't get to sleep last night. I think the trouble started with the shots."

He glanced over again. "We said we'd come down here and give it a chance."

Silence hung between them. Sam turned and looked into his eyes, staring at him for a moment as Jack continued: "I'm trying. You still on board?"

She nodded her head, then leaned in and kissed him softly, "Of course I am. You dream about me last night?"

Jack smiled and said, "Sure."

"Have a good time?"

"Yeah… so'd you," he replied.

She smiled and settled back, her eyes focused on a sign on the shoulder that announced, "Antelope Wells Border Inspection Station, 3 miles."

***

In the distance, a rundown building with a corrugated metal roof squatted in the sweltering heat.

A man wearing a wife-beater t-shirt and ball cap leaned against the side of a pick-up. Polarized aviator-style sunglasses shielded his eyes from the bright morning sun. He wasn't quite six feet tall - slim, well built with a soul patch under his bottom lip. He was wearing jeans and cowboy boots.

His gaze followed the Cherokee as it pulled into the parking lot of the rundown gas station and rolled to a stop in front of a small market.

A couple of bikers sat between the pumps revving their engines, waiting to take off.

As they climbed out of the Cherokee, Sam grabbed her backpack.

Jack's eyes flicked past her to one of the bikers, and the biker glanced back. For an instant, their eyes locked.

The biker nodded, a hint of a smile twisting his lips. He gave one of those nods, like "I know you." Jack warily nodded.

The man leaning against the pick-up continued to watch them with an impassive face.

Sam looked at him. A moment passed between them; then, she looked back at Jack. "I'll see ya in a minute," she called back to him as she continued around the side of the market and disappeared from view.

Jack opened the screen door of the market and walked inside.

The place was empty and blistering hot. Jack got his bearings as he made his way through the market.

A ceiling fan slowly turned above the suffocating heat. The Ed Sullivan Show with "Topo Gigio" droned from a TV.

A man sat behind the register eating a burrito. He spoke into the phone in Spanish while watching Jack approach.

He caught an old woman looking at him. She was waving herself with a hand fan, trying to stay cool.

Jack looked at her with a good-natured smile and said, "Morning."

The woman glared at him. She didn't understand English, and she didn't like Gabachos either.

Jack paid for two coffees a few minutes later, exchanging pleasantries with the proprietor in broken Spanish.

He looked around the room. Something was bothering him, but Jack didn't know what it was. He looked back out the front window at the Cherokee.

Sam wasn't back yet.

Jack pushed open the screen door and moved toward the Cherokee, looking around. The bikers were gone, so was the pick-up. The only other vehicle in the parking lot was a black, late model Chrysler 300.

He set the coffees on the hood of the Cherokee, then glanced back at the market.

Dim light shined through a dirty window from inside a small, rundown restroom.

Jack called out, "Sam, are you okay?"

A beat later, the door to the disgusting bathroom swung open. Light spilled in from outside as Jack leaned in. "Sam?"

Brutal silence was broken by the water-torture-like sound of dripping in the rust-stained sink and the muffled sound of the Mexican music playing inside the market.

Jack stood there, trying to process the situation. He had trouble breathing when he found nothing but his own image staring back at him from the cracked mirror above the chipped porcelain sink.

A beat later, he was gone.

***

He looked in every direction during a dead run toward the Cherokee. He shouted, "Samantha?!" Still, no Sam.

Jack started to panic and began to move back toward the market. Suddenly a cell phone rang.

He recognized that ringtone. It was Sam's.

Jack sprinted back to the Cherokee, reached inside, and picked it up. "Where are you?"

A man's voice answered. "Some vacation, huh?"

"Who is this?! You listen to me, if…"

The man's voice interrupted, "If you ever want to see her again, don't talk. Listen."

Jack tried to maintain his composure as the man's voice continued, "Are you listening to me, Jack?"

Jack hesitated for a moment, then coldly asked, "How do you know my name?"

"Keys are in the ignition. You've got five hours to drive to Gallup."

Jack started to lose it. "What are you talking about?! I'm not leaving Sam!"

"You have nothing to worry about as long as you do what you're told."

Jack hesitated, then said, "Gallup is an eight-hour drive."

"I love New Mexico. Where else can you travel a thousand miles in just under eight hours? You've got five. Do we understand each other, Jack?"

The line went dead.

Jack stood there for a moment, his head spinning, feeling like the most helpless man alive. Sweat glistened on his face. He looked back at the Chrysler.

CHAPTER 2

With a deafening roar, the black Chrysler 300S Hemi crossed the desert like a straight line on Route 81 and approached the United States/Mexico border.

Traffic was light until Jack drew within sight of the Antelope Wells Inspection Station. It was the smallest border crossing of the forty-seven points between the United States and Mexico.

He shot a quick glance at the digital clock on the dash. There was more traffic on the road now.

After a few minutes, he was waved through Mexican customs. Boxed in by trees on the right and left, Jack slowed as he approached the U.S. side of customs.

His eyes never stopped moving - Jack couldn't believe what he was doing. He chanced a look at his wristwatch - ten o'clock.

Ahead, a couple of cars waited to cross. Custom agents diligently checked each driver's I.D. closely against information on their clipboards.

Jack continued to scan the people, perspiration soaking his face. A customs agent leading a German Shepard walked toward him.

He caught a glimpse of a woman moving away from him. Was it Sam? She moved in and out of view amongst the other pedestrians.

She glanced back. It wasn't Sam. Just another American tourist.

Further ahead on the opposite side, U.S. customs agents checked vehicles as they passed through into Mexico.

Jack's gaze flashed to the rearview as another car pulled up behind him.

Ahead, the red light turned green, and a customs agent waved the first car through. Another agent pointed at the vehicle in front of Jack and motioned for the driver to pull into the holding area. Security was on high alert.

***

Another agent sat in front of a bank of monitors in a featureless room, watching intently as a dozen security cameras captured everything.

A televised newscast broke the silence, the anchorman sharing: "Security has been on high alert this week at all the airports along the international border between the United States and Mexico, as FAA, in concert with Federal Officials, have expanded the virtual lockdown of all private air traffic in the area."

As the reporter droned on with his running commentary, he explained that State and Federal officials had responded to a breach in security at the state prison in Juarez earlier in the week. One inmate and two Federal officials were killed during a fierce battle between rival cartel gangs. A circumstance that resulted in the failed extradition and untimely escape of Daniel Martin, who was still believed to be in the state of Chihuahua.

***

Jack rolled to a stop, the agent glanced down at her clipboard, looking between a mug shot of Daniel Martin and Jack.

Jack noticed another agent looking at him and asked the woman at the window, "Is there a problem?"

The agent looked up from the clipboard and said, "I.D."

Jack handed her his passport.

"Anything to declare?"

"No, ma'am," Jack replied.

"How long were you in Mexico?"

"Just a couple of days," Jack answered.

"Business or pleasure?" the border agent asked, looking down at Jack.

"Pleasure."

***

Positioned on an overpass in the distance, the man in the wife-beater T-shirt stood next to his pick-up, watching Jack through a pair of binoculars.

He could see the entire inspection station spread out below him from the bridge. He panned from Jack to another car parked at the curb next to the Chrysler and adjusted the focus until he could see the driver clearly.

He watched through the binoculars as the driver answered a cell phone call. "Hola," a voice said.

The man spoke into his cell phone, voice calm: "Hello, my friend. We good?"

The driver nodded. "Yes, amigo."

***

Jack looked around, then up at the rearview. He started to breathe a little heavier and quietly said to the agent, "Listen, I've got a little..." Suddenly, from his lap, Sam's cell phone began to ring.

The agent looked down as the phone continued to ring. "You want to answer that, sir?"

Jack shrugged an apology. "Thanks," he replied as he turned away to answer. "Yeah?"

"It's a brave new world, Jack," the man's voice said. "I thought we understood each other."

"I miss you too, honey." Jack's eyes shifted, unwilling to believe what he was seeing. His eyes locked on a tiny lipstick camera mounted next to the visor, then flicked toward another on the dash.

***

In the blackness, a split screen of six live, real-time feeds played on a monitor, displaying multiple images. Camera angles outside, ahead, and behind the Chrysler followed Jack's every movement - making automatic lens corrections.

***

"C'mon, Jack. This is one of those rare moments when you get a chance to be completely honest."

Jack reluctantly nodded as the man's voice continued: "Tell me straight. You do love this girl, don't you?"

Jack was speechless.

***

Jack's voice and the customs agent's reply were heard in the blackness: "You okay, sir?"

***

"Yeah, I'm fine. Just my girl wondering when I'm going to be home."

The agent slowly extended the man's passport in his direction. Something wasn't right. She looked at Jack for a moment. After an endless pause, she asked, "How long have you been married?"

Jack quickly took control and changed the tone, "We're not. She's my girlfriend."

Jack's sixth sense tweaked as he looked over and made eye contact with the driver of the car parked next to him.

His eyes flicked up to the rearview, and he spotted another agent moving toward the trunk of the Chrysler.

Suddenly, the driver next to him slammed his car into gear and stomped on the gas, pulling away from the curb and racing toward the holding area. A split second later, he slammed into the back of a parked car, which was knocked sideways into a row of border patrol cars.

A flock of birds exploded out of the trees. There was a whirlwind of activity as personnel began to swarm the area.

The agent waved Jack through. "Go ahead, sir."

"Yeah, have a nice day," Jack said under his breath.

"A nice day," the caller echoed. "Pretty this time of year, too. Better buckle up, Jack." Then the line went dead.

***

Thirty minutes later, the Chrysler was roaring along smoothly, hitting over a hundred miles per hour. Jack passed a couple of slower moving vehicles and a billboard which read: "Welcome to New Mexico, The Land of Enchantment."

The GPS chirped as it connected, "Take the first right onto Route 146, 19.1 miles to Interstate 10, east to Deming 32.2 miles."

Jack leaned forward and turned it off. He continued to stare straight ahead at the empty highway. It gave him time to think about the last eight hours, which started in a nightclub just outside Nuevo Casa Grandes.

***

The energy was intense, and the packed dance floor was on fire. Jack and Sam had been in the middle of it dirty dancing.

Jack looked like a hunter who spotted a piece of big game.

Sam saw him, and kind of laughed when their eyes met. She stared at him, cocked a finger – aimed it like a gun right between his eyes - and pantomimed pulling the trigger.

He feigned innocence and said, "Ouch."

They both laughed as she danced for him and shouted over the music, "Do you ever wish you could be with someone else and not me?"

Later, as they sat at the bar, "Easy to be Hard" by Three Dog Night droned from the pre-sixties jukebox. The place was half empty.

Jack toasted Sam with a shot of tequila, "Why would you ask me that?" he questioned after they both downed the shots. "Do you?"

Sam didn't answer, staring at an arguing couple seated directly across from them. Solemnly, she shook her head "no."

Jack smiled to himself and said, "How sweet it is."

He managed a little smile from her. She looked over at him, their eyes met, and Jack smiled. "We deserve more."

***

The first light of dawn washed over him as he slept in the front seat of the Cherokee.

The side door was open, and a mangy dog sniffed and licked his face as Jack woke with a start. He sat up and looked around as the dog jumped down and ran away.

There was little sign of life when Jack called, "Sam?"

Then he spotted her, watching from a distance. After a beat, Sam slowly walked toward the Jeep.

"Hi," he said.

She smiled and replied, "Good morning."

"What are you doing? How long have you been up?"

"'Bout fifteen minutes." She climbed in and studied his face.

"C'mon, I don't feel as bad as I look. You look great," he said.

They both sat there for a moment, "There's something on your mind? What is it?" he asked.

Sam didn't answer; instead, she stared out the windshield.

He studied her in silence, then said, "C'mere."

Sam shook her head and leaned against his shoulder.

After a couple of seconds, he quietly said, "I guess we better get going."

Snapping back to the present, Jack put aside the memory, stared straight ahead, and told himself to breathe.

There was no traffic on the road - nothing going his way. And nothing going the other way.

He took a deep breath and accelerated.

***

The sun was brutal - heat rippled across the flat white desert in a hallucinogenic wave.

A red-tailed hawk enjoyed a bit of roadkill in the middle of Route 146.

In the distance, the black Chrysler screamed across the deserted highway, heading toward a run-down diner.

There wasn't much life there - just one car parked in front.

Inside the greasy spoon, it was hot and smelled of coffee. The only sound came from an ancient television on the wall facing the counter. A lone customer sat at the counter watching the TV as the running news commentary continued, "American educated, fluent in over a dozen languages, Martin is now the subject of an international manhunt."

A photo of Daniel Martin's chiseled and intelligent features filled the screen. He was in his late-40's, his dark hair combed straight back.

The customer continued nursing his cup of coffee as the Chrysler flashed by outside.

***

Jack pushed the car faster, his eyes fixed on the road ahead.

He quickly closed on an eighteen-wheeler, which effectively limited his view ahead. He pulled out to pass, saw it was clear, and accelerated.

Sling-shotting past the semi, the Chrysler dropped back in front of it, and Jack glanced up at the rearview.

Directly behind him was a New Mexico State Trooper. He glanced in the side mirror as the cruiser began closing in, lights flashing.

Jack shook his head and pulled over.

The State Trooper got out of his cruiser and walked toward Jack.

Jack rolled his window down and looked up. The glaring sun momentarily obscured the Trooper's face.

"You were speedin' pretty good back there, sir."

"Yeah, sorry about that," Jack said. "Just trying to take the shot when I had it."

"License and registration, please."

Jack reached for his wallet, pulled out his license, and handed it to the officer.

"And registration, please."

Jack didn't move.

"Maybe it's in the glove compartment, sir."

Jack nodded, popped it open, and pulled out the registration. He hesitated for a moment, then handed it to the officer.

The Trooper looked at Jack's license, then at Jack, then at the registration for a couple of seconds. Finally, he looked back at Jack.

"Thank you, Mr. Mathews.

Jack controlled himself with an effort, straightened, and said very conversationally, "Excuse me, sir? What'd you say?"

The Trooper turned back. "I said, thank you, Mr. Mathews."

***

In the blackness, the visuals and audio of Jack and the Trooper played on the screens:

"Yeah, right. Excuse me. I'm sorry, officer."

"Just remain in the car, please."

Jack watched the Trooper walk away in the side mirror. After what seemed like an eternity, he returned and handed him his license, then the registration.

"Next time, try to follow the speed limit, Mr. Mathews."

"Thank you, officer," Jack said.

The Trooper nodded, "Drive carefully."

"You too, officer."

Jack started the Chrysler, put it in gear, and pulled away as he watched the cruiser in the rearview.

Minutes later, engine roaring, going sixty, and picking up speed, Sam's cell rang again. Jack brought it up to his ear as the man's voice spoke, "That was quite a performance back there."

Jack held the registration up in front of the camera next to the visor, "What's this? What's my name doing on it?"

"A little gift for you and your lady when this is all over."

Jack's face remained cold, expressionless.

"Do you mind if I ask you something personal?" After a beat, the voice questioned, "You ever cheat on a woman?"

"What?! What the hell are you talking about?"

"Did you? I don't mean to pry," the man said.

"Then don't."

"I can understand your reluctance to tell… you wanna think about it?"

"Why are you doing this? Are you insane?" Jack replied.

"You better pick it up, Jack."

The line went dead again.

Frustrated, Jack said, "Hey Google, put on Sirius XM Traffic Plus." He began to listen to real-time traffic information and formulate alternate routes.

He looked at his watch…11:30.

CHAPTER 3

Traffic began to back up on the eastbound lanes of Interstate 10. State Troopers had positioned their vehicles to funnel traffic into one lane at a checkpoint.

The pick-up slowed down. All they could see were brake lights, and the man in the wife-beater T-shirt glanced around nice and easy. His gaze shifted to the Troopers, who stopped each car and checked their trunks.

He tried to decide whether to continue forward or pull out of line as another car pulled in behind him.

Sam, wearing sunglasses, glanced over at him as he picked up a cell phone and hit speed dial.

In the Chrysler, Jack brought Sam's cell phone up to his ear as the man's voice spoke: "Change in plans. Take exit 82A, then get back on at 82B."

"How do I know she's still alive?" Jack asked.

The line went dead.

When the pick-up rolled to a stop at the checkpoint, a State Trooper leaned in and glanced at the man, then Sam. Sam looked over as the Trooper waved them through.

Jack's cell rang; caught off guard, he reached for it and answered.

"Jack?"

"Sam! Where are you?!"

"Jack, just do what they say."

"I love you," he said.

"I love you, too, Jack."

"Tell me later," he said. Then the line went dead.

Jack recovered his composure, looked up at the 82A exit sign, and accelerated.

The Chrysler flew past a parked cruiser as the State Trooper looked up from his radar gun - just in time to catch a glimpse of the Chrysler as it cut across traffic and slid into the right lane, barely making the offramp. The gun was flashing 100 mph.

Seconds later, the Chrysler continued to weave in and out of traffic through downtown Deming. Horns blared, and pedestrians scattered as it sliced through cross traffic.

Jack blew through another red light. Cars crashed. He stayed calm, glancing in his rearview at the intersection behind him. Engine roaring, he continued to pass and weave around the stunned drivers. He swung the Chrysler into the opposite lane to get around slower moving traffic, shot through another red light, then glanced in the rearview at the car he just missed colliding with. Overtaking slower traffic, Jack sped back up the eastbound 82B onramp.

He bypassed the checkpoint, then wiped his forehead with his arm. He mumbled "shit" under his breath and smiled. Jack was amazed he could smile at anything at this point, but he did. His grin faltered a bit as he glanced down at Sam's cell phone.

Something caught his attention ahead: sirens wailing. A sea of flashing lights fastly approached in the westbound lanes. Jack didn't blink as three cruisers shot past, going the opposite direction.

Sam's cell rang again. Jack answered it.

The man's voice was very agitated and getting edgy. "What the hell was that! Are you fucking crazy?!"

"Just trying to stay focused. What was I supposed to do?" Jack said.

There was a long pause; then the man finally answered: "You've just blown the one thing you had going in your favor. It won't be long before they'll be coming after you."

Jack said nothing as the man continued, "Your only chance is to outrun them before they catch up with you."

"This shit is crazy. Who the fuck are you?!" Jack shouted, "And where is Sam? This is bullshit!!"

"It's not bullshit if you want to see her again." After a pause, he added, "Alright then? No hard feelings. Don't stop until you get to Gallup. Understand? Your number one priority is to get there by three o'clock."

"If you touch her, I'll kill you."

"No faith in our newfound friendship, Jack?"

Enough, Jack thought. He hung up, reached over, and turned the radio on. The Black Keys' "Weight of Love" began to blare from the surrounds.

A thumping bass built as a police helicopter rose in silhouette, its rotors strobing in the sunlight. Inside, the pilot keyed his mic, "All units, be advised: air unit five is in pursuit of a late model black Chrysler. Suspect is believed to be heading eastbound on Interstate 10."

Up ahead, the man and Sam watched a cruiser as it roared past them - Sam's sunglasses reflecting the flashing lights on the cruiser as a second cruiser dropped in behind it. The police helicopter flashed overhead, thumping its way down the interstate, closing in on the Chrysler.

Jack pushed the vehicle toward 100 mph, blowing through traffic.

***

In blackness, the feeds from the six cameras continued to play.

***

The clock on the wall of the KTEG radio station read twelve o'clock. A police scanner blared in the background.

As "Weight of Love" ended, the D.J., seated behind the glass, began to gesture wildly in front of his microphone. Then he calmly said, "Here we go again. Some guy has launched a shitstorm of his own out there…."

Jack stared straight ahead as he listened to the broadcast.

"I'm getting reports of another high-speed pursuit. This guy's rock'n it in a black Chrysler, eastbound on Interstate 10. Does anybody out there ever wonder how much this shit cost?"

The Chrysler roared along the shoulder doing eighty. Jack passed slower traffic, their horns blaring as drivers swerved out of the way.

"This is 'Shred,' sitting in for Baxter. It's good to be back at KTEG, 104.1, The Edge."

Jack looked over at the cruiser that paced him on the frontage road, which paralleled the interstate, as Shred continued, "Who's behind the wheel? Why's he running?"

The police helicopter appeared alongside the Chrysler, rotors thumping as it dropped in closer. The pilot held steady and kept pace with the Chrysler as he keyed his mic. "We have suspect vehicle matching description of a black, late model Chrysler, License 4PDC654, over."

The spotter next to the pilot focused his telescopic viewfinder on Jack.

The dispatcher's voice broke in, "Is it Daniel Martin?"

The spotter shook his head "no."

Shred continued to listen to the scanner as a technician, R.T. - a portly Indian in his late twenties, hair cut short, or 'bobtailed,' as the Indians say - came into the booth.

The pilot's voice broke in again, "Negative. I don't think it's our boy, over."

Shred glanced up at R.T. and asked, "Who the hell is Daniel Martin?"

R.T. opened his laptop. "Hold on; I'll find out."

The dispatcher's voice came over the scanner: "All units. A rolling roadblock is being executed at exit 93. Be advised; the suspect is traveling in excess of 100 mph."

***

The pick-up traveled with the flow of traffic. In the distance, they could see brake lights as traffic began to slow again. Both occupants' thoughts were lost in separate worlds.

As traffic continued to slow, they could see the flashing lights of the rolling roadblock ahead. Suddenly, the Chrysler sling-shot past them on the shoulder.

The helicopter overhead banked sharply - the changing pitch of the turbines and rotors chopped the air - as it rapidly descended, following the Chrysler down the offramp. The pilot keyed his mic again, "Suspect has exited Interstate 10 at exit 93, proceeding north on the frontage road."

The Chrysler dropped onto the frontage road and roared through the intersection. Jack checked his rearview as the cruiser, lights flashing, dropped right in on his ass. Both vehicles continued to pass the slower traffic.

***

Without looking up, R.T. Googled Daniel Martin on his laptop and said, "Very little is known about the globe-trotting mastermind known as 'The Specialist.' U.S. intelligence agencies have determined, although assumed, he is the architect of a 60 million dollar Ponzi scheme in 2016, in addition to two others in 2020 and 2021."

Shred swiveled around in his chair and faced R.T. as he continued.

"…until recently, his very existence was in question. Multiple fake identities and falsified backgrounds." R.T. looked up. "And then he pulled his vanishing act."

***

Jack glanced out the side window at the helicopter that kept pace with him; then, he looked back at the road in front of him as more sirens rose behind him. Three more cruisers exited the interstate and dropped in behind the cruiser that chased him.

Coming up fast on traffic, Jack's eyes flicked up to the rearview. There was a blurry wall of red and blue flashing lights, their sirens growing louder.

Adrenaline pumping, he pulled out to pass, but horns blared, and he veered back just in time, barely missing an oncoming car. His eyes locked on the U-Haul tow-behind trailer directly in front of him. "Fuck it!" Jack smashed the gas pedal, slicing across head-on traffic, which caused a chain reaction.

As he crossed in front of the first car, the semi tractor-trailer driver behind it slammed on his air-brakes, over-compensating as the rig began to jack-knife.

The driver towing the U-Haul trailer panicked and slammed on his brakes as the semi trailer swung out in front of him.

Jack struggled to maintain control on the shoulder. As the Chrysler flashed past the semi, the first cruiser slammed into the rear end of the U-Haul trailer. In an eruption of glass and metal, the cruiser was spit into the air, doing a lazy spin before coming down hard. The second cruiser locked up, spun out of control, and slammed into the first as the third brutally T-boned it.

The Chrysler left the shoulder, slicing through oncoming traffic, then swerved back onto the road. Jack cursed under his breath as he slowed with the flow of traffic.

The helicopter flared up as the pilot keyed his mic: "Pursuit has been terminated." The pilot hovered directly over the carnage, his rotors chopping the air as he prepared to land. Keying his mic again, he said, "We've got multiple T.A.'s, with multiple injuries. We need immediate emergency response, over."

CHAPTER 4

Chris Stapleton's "You Should Probably Leave" played from the surround sound system as the fourth cruiser appeared behind them, closing fast. Instantly, Jack used a diversionary tactic: as the cruiser was about to hit his ass-end, he stomped on the parking brake. The Chrysler spun on the straight - into a screeching spin - out braking the cruiser. Then Jack took a hard right, leaving the cruiser hydroplaning behind him on all four wheels as it slid off the street and slammed into a parked car.

Jack corrected, accelerated out of the turn, and blew through traffic. He glanced in the rearview and seemed calm in spite of what just happened; he couldn't help but smile to himself as he settled back into his seat.

***

The music continued to play in the background as R.T. cued up the next selection from the playlist on his laptop. He noticed the phone board light up with a call and lightly knocked on the wall of the glass booth behind him and mouthed, "Got one on three."

Shred picked up the call. "KTEG. This is Shred. Speak."

"Digger, from Santa Fe," the caller said.

"Where are you calling from, brother?"

"Just outside Las Cruces, I was on my way back into town when your boy caused quite a mess out here. We're talking 'Jaws of Life' mess. This guy's book'n it, man. They've gotta bag this dude."

"And you're alright?" Shred asked.

"Oh, hell yeah. It was like some kamikaze-suicide shit. But I'm alive, got it made in the shade, amigo."

"Bet'chu do, Digger. Appreciate you calling in." Intrigued, Shred hung up and looked up at R.T.

***.

Jack looked up at the rearview. For the moment, the cruisers and the helicopter were gone.

Almost like a mirage in the heat waves coming off the highway, the Chrysler swung off the asphalt and screamed down a rough, two-track dirt road. Less than a half a mile from the highway, the road got rougher. The Chrysler screeched to a stop. Jack turned off the radio then looked up at the tiny camera next to the visor.

***

In the blackness, the six feeds played in real time on the monitor. Jack continued to look into the camera. "I have to piss," he said.

Jack left the engine running as he got out and walked to the rear of the Chrysler. On another camera angle, Jack stopped with his back to the vehicle. Behind him, dust devils chased themselves.

Jack glanced back at the Chrysler.

After a couple of seconds, all the screens went black.

***

A dry breeze whisked up the dust at Jack's feet as he zipped up. Something seemed wrong. He glanced out at the open space, then back at the Chrysler again. Stunned, he froze where he stood.

His eyes focused on something he couldn't have anticipated - the Chrysler's rear deck lid was wide open.

Jack wiped the sweat from his eyes and took a cautious step forward, his gaze transfixed on the open trunk. Inside it had all the comforts of home: it was retrofitted with a completely padded eight-point mini roll cage, designed for maximum safety and comfort. A carbon fiber seat with a restraint system was attached to bungee cords, which were attached to four pick-points on the cage. Behind it, a twenty-four-inch black monitor screen was secured to the cage.

Jack slammed the trunk lid shut and looked up at the silhouette of a figure sitting in the passenger seat. Stunned by the reality of the situation, he slowly moved forward and continued around to the driver's side.

The figure turned and looked up at him; his eyes were cold. He smiled at Jack like he had all the time in the world, then said, "Do you know who I am, Jack?"

Jack's eyes were wide as he stared at Daniel Martin.

"Where's Sam?" he asked.

Martin brought up a 9mm and leveled it at him, "Easy. Get in the car, Jack."

"I'm not going anywhere until you tell me what's going on," Jack replied.

Something flashed in Martin's eyes, and for a second, Jack wasn't sure where the situation was going.

Martin looked around after a very tense moment. "Get in the fucking car, Jack."

"Where is she? Go ahead and shoot me; I don't give a shit!" Jack said.

Martin just shook his head, "Why are you so anxious to die?" Silence hung in the air, then, "Well?"

"You giving me a choice?" Jack answered.

"If you test my resolve, then God help you. You're on my good side, and I think you want to stay there. Now get in the fucking car and drive."

Jack's eyes burned with rage, but slowly that rage changed. A strange smile came to his face as Martin continued, "Were you trying to get us both killed back there?"

Jack refused to reply as he climbed in behind the wheel.

Suddenly, Martin slammed Jack's face down against the steering wheel in one quick move. "You move, you die… what can I say. I won't ask again. So, don't fuck with me, huh?"

Jack slowly looked up over at him and replied, "No?"

"Are you disrespecting me, Jack? Is that what you're doing?" Martin said as he released him.

They just stared each other down.

Jack sat there for a moment, then turned and stared out the side window.

"Well, Jack. What's it going to be? I don't have much time."

Jack paused, then took a deep breath and exhaled. He made his decision. And he gave Martin his answer as he slammed the car into low gear and stomped on the gas. The speedometer pegged at zero as the car screamed backward. Cranking the wheel, Jack spun the Chrysler 180 degrees, then stomped on the gas again - whipping back onto the road at 80 mph and climbing.

Martin sat silent and still, staring straight ahead. After a couple of seconds, he turned to Jack and studied him with cold eyes. "Are you fucking with me, Jack? Or are you done fucking with me?" Then, almost to himself, he said, "You're becoming more trouble than you're worth."

The strangeness of the situation didn't amuse Jack; he shook his head and said, "In the trunk the whole time."

"I'm very resilient. Kinda like Gumby," Martin said as he took out a burner phone and tossed it out the window. Then he checked his watch. "Right on time."

***

Shred watched the local news feed of the carnage on the frontage road unfold: the road was choked with smoke, flashing lights, and emergency vehicles. A Med-a-vac helicopter approached in the distance. On each side of the accident site, blockades of State Cruisers had been established.

"Eyewitness-7 News on the scene. Just minutes ago, a high-speed pursuit ended with a deadly conclusion. We want to warn viewers that the images you are seeing are very graphic, and viewer discretion is advised. The most recent information we have from police is that they have identified the suspect as Jack Mathews. Police speculation is that he may be headed north."

R.T. glanced at Shred. "Hey, you gotta check this out. It's the only known photograph of him."

As the news anchor continued, Shred got up and walked out of the booth.

"… roadblocks are being established on Interstate 25, just south of Albuquerque."

Shred leaned in and studied Jack's image on the laptop. "Jack Mathews. I want to know everything there is to know about him." Then he walked back into the booth and cued up Tom Petty's "Runnin' Down a Dream." As it began to play, he looked out at R.T. "Can you imagine the feeding frenzy of the media? You can practically taste the brain matter."

***

Jack kept his eyes on the road - there was no traffic, and the sky was clear of clouds.

After minutes of silent tension, Martin looked over at Jack, then around as he admired the car's interior. "Made in America. Nice, huh?" His gaze swung back to Jack. "The thing of it is, it's just a question of logistics. This is gonna work if you make it work." Martin waited for a response. Nothing. "You know what makes the world go round, Jack?"

Jack glanced at Martin. "No, tell me."

"Money."

"Some people say love," Jack said.

Martin smiled. "It is love. The love of money."

As Jack looked over, Martin motioned with the 9mm for him to keep his eyes on the road. "There are three types of people in the world, Jack: those who make it happen, those who watch it happen, and those who say what happened." After a beat, he questioned, "Which one are you?"

Jack just stared straight ahead and remained silent.

"We both want the same thing here. The only way to deal with this is to take me where I want to go."

"And then what?" Jack questioned.

"She lives." Martin glanced out the window. "Funny how differently things look depending on where you sit."

***

R.T. pulled up a picture of two people on his laptop. Shred leaned in for a closer look. "Who's the chick?" he asked.

"That's Martin and his wife."

Shred studied the woman's face.

***

The man glanced over at Sam as the pick-up transitioned from Interstate 10 in Las Cruces to Interstate 25. Sam continued to stare straight ahead, lost in thought, thinking about the previous evening at the nightclub —

As their eyes met, Jack smiled and said, "We deserve more."

She nodded her head as if listening to him. She glanced up at the mirror behind the bar, tracking someone across the room behind them.

The figure stopped. A match flared as the man lit a cigarette and watched them, his eyes on Sam. He nodded in apparent recognition, with an understanding smile on his face. The match went out; then, his face faded to black.

She faintly smiled to herself and looked back at Jack, who was watching her.

He scrutinized her for a second, then downed a shot and said, "Surprise me sometime, okay? Can you do that? Tell me what you're actually thinking."

Caught, she had no answer for that. Without missing a beat, she turned to Jack and whispered, "What do you think?" Then she rose abruptly, ready to walk out.

Jack bolted off his barstool, laughing, making light of it. He saw she was serious, "Okay, it was a dumb question," he said.

She laughed. Fuck it, she thought.

Jack motioned at the bartender for 'two more shots.'

The man continued to watch them for a moment, then turned and walked out.

Jack leaned in and asked, "Do you know how much I love you?"

She smiled warmly and cocked her head. "No, tell me."

"Okay, I love you."

The two of them slow danced to Cesaria Evora's "Crepuscular Solidao" as the night wound down. Jack's eyes were closed. He appeared to be wasted, his head in the song. He softly said, "Dearly beloved, we are gathered here… forget that shit, just say, 'I do.'"

Jack looked at Sam, their faces inches apart. Each read the other's eyes as he continued, "Just want to see if I'm with the person you say you are.

Can't be too careful."

Without looking up, she said, "Me?" Her eyes slowly came up, hesitant, then playful. "Don't give me that shit." She put her arms around his neck. Jack slid his arms around her waist, and he kissed her. When he pulled back, she was staring at him as if at a loss for something to say.

He studied her for a beat, then said, "Well?"

She slowly nodded her head "yes."

He looked around at the empty nightclub. "Anybody object?"

For a long moment, Jack held her, their eyes locked. She leaned closer, the sexual tension strong. After a moment, the two very slowly kissed deeply and passionately.

Sam's eyes blinked back to the present. She appeared overwhelmed, then looked over at the man who watched her.

He kinda smiled. But the smile passed as quickly as it came before he switched the A.C. to high.

CHAPTER 5

The Chrysler roared down a long stretch of highway, some two hundred fifty miles south of Gallup. The only sound was the steady hum of the engine.

Martin glanced at his watch; it was 1:30. He looked up at Jack, who was glaring at him.

"How many innocent people are gonna die before this is over?" Jack asked.

Martin pulled out another burner phone and activated the sim card. As the cell started to beep, he answered it, listened for a couple of seconds, then said, "I know." He hung up and glanced at Jack again. "Change in plans. You ever been to Truth or Consequences?"

"I want to talk to Sam."

"Soon, Jack. Just Drive."

Jack turned on the radio. "Runnin' Down a Dream" filled the surrounds; Martin reached forward and turned it down.

***

The music played in the background as R.T. looked up from his laptop. "You're not going to believe this." Shred glanced over as he continued. "Went on Facebook," he said as he double-clicked. "Check out Jack's girlfriend."

Shred stared at a picture of Jack and Sam. "Pull up Martin and his wife again." They looked at each other, then back at the screen. The same woman was in both pictures.

***

The music wound down as the Chrysler roared past the mesas. Shred's voice came on: "Crazy stuff, huh? Listen, speaking of crazy stuff? That high-speed pursuit? The guy's name is Jack Mathews. That's not all. Turns out his girlfriend is…"

Martin reached up and turned off the radio. "You're getting famous; you know that? All over the goddam news."

Jack considered it for a moment, then simply said, "Yeah. So are you going to talk me to death?"

"Maybe you'll understand this." Martin leveled the gun at Jack's head. "You gonna fuck with me again, Jack? Decide. Before it gets decided for you."

Jack shook his head 'no,' then stomped on the gas. The Chrysler rocketed forward.

"Alright, slow down," Martin said.

But Jack wasn't letting up, 80… 90…

Yelling over the engine, Martin leaned in and pressed the barrel of the 9mm against the side of Jack's head. "Slow the fuck down!" But the speed kept increasing - 100…120…

Jack was remarkably calm, considering his predicament. He started to say something but thought better of it.

"So, shall we discuss it in a civilized manner?" Martin questioned. "Is there a point you're trying to make?"

"Where's Sam?"

"Now you're insulting me."

Jack said nothing.

"Well?"

"Yeah. Whatever," Jack replied.

"Too bad, Jack. Guess you gotta go."

"You pull the trigger, we both die," Jack said.

"We'll see." Martin started to pull the trigger.

"Wait!"

"Maybe we're beginning to understand each other, huh? Blink twice fast for yes."

Jack blinked twice, fast, and let off the gas.

Martin lowered the gun. "I was just fucking with you, Jack."

Jack quickly recovered and met Martin's scrutinizing gaze. Then

Jack gave him a 'fuck you' smile. "So was I."

"In which case, we're way past that. Don't you think?" Martin said as he settled back in his seat.

Jack glanced over at him. "I guess sooner or later you're gonna explain all this, huh?"

Martin continued to stare through the front windshield as he smiled to himself and pulled out the burner phone.

***

"I understand," the man said. Sam looked over at him as he hung up his cell phone. "Seems your boy is becoming a liability."

She laughed, giving her tension a release. "How bad can it be?"

"You have no idea," the man said.

She appeared pensive, then looked away out the side window.

"You okay?" he asked.

"Sure. You?" she replied.

***

The Chrysler continued to roar along smoothly. "Okay, Mr. Celebrity?" Martin said as he pointed up ahead at a billboard that announced "Truth or Consequences, City of Elephant Butte."

"Time to say goodbye to our ride; let's go shopping."

They drove in silence as they rolled into downtown Truth or Consequences. The Chrysler slowed to a crawl as it continued down the main street.

Jack glanced over at Martin, who checked his watch as he looked out the side window at the vintage WWII buildings. Several Indians had their wares laid out on the sidewalk. Tourists wandered. Martin looked impatient, his eyes searching.

Ahead, a group of children played. A mother jumped out of a waiting van and ran over to them.

Martin shook his head 'no.' "Keep driving."

Jack stopped at a red light.

"You should learn a little patience."

"Is that right?" Jack questioned.

Martin looked out the side window again and continued to stare at a row of cars in a used car lot. "It's considered a virtue by some."

"Yeah? Well, not me right now." Ahead the light turned green. Jack checked the rearview, and he continued across the intersection.

The Chrysler continued down the main street. As they crossed another intersection, a Police SUV turned onto the street and dropped in about five or six car lengths behind them.

Jack clocked the SUV in the mirror. He stayed calm as he rechecked the rearview. The SUV turned off onto a side street. False alarm. He relaxed and laughed to himself.

"What's so funny?" Martin asked.

Jack didn't answer. But after a beat, he replied, "If this is going to happen, it's gotta happen now."

"Patience, Jack."

Jack wasn't listening as he glanced in his side mirror. Nothing. Then he looked over at Martin and said, "C'mon, man, maybe this wasn't such a good idea."

Jack noticed people on the sidewalk eyeing them, his paranoia rising. He swore under his breath as another police car turned onto the street ahead of them.

"Easy," Martin said.

The police car continued toward them. As it passed by, going the opposite direction, Jack made eye contact with the two cops and focused on the driver - a hard stare between them.

He checked his rearview again, watching the cruiser as it slowly continued up the street. Finally, It turned the corner and disappeared from view.

Jack sighed in relief as he looked at the intersection ahead of them. His eyes flicked in all directions, then up at the mirror again. Nothing.

Woop-woop!

He whipped the Chrysler around the corner and accelerated. Suddenly, he heard a siren a few blocks away, then another even closer. "Shit," he said to himself.

Martin looked over. "Feeling lucky?"

"Not particularly, no," Jack replied. They both looked back at the police car bearing down on them.

"What are you waiting for? Go!" Martin shouted.

Jack hesitated, his eyes locked on the police car in his rearview.

"Drive, or I'll blow your fuckin' head off!"

Jack dumped the car into low gear as the Chrysler came alive.

The two cars screamed down the street.

The driver of the police car keyed his mic: "In pursuit of two suspects in a black Chrysler matching the description of the vehicle sought in connection with the high-speed chase in Las Cruces. Suspects are headed north on Solano Drive."

The Chrysler skidded around a corner and knifed in front of another police car, which joined the pursuit. Jack was driving hard, pushing the car through traffic. Curious pedestrians recorded the Chrysler on their cell phones as it blew past them, followed by the two police cruisers.

The Chrysler crossed an intersection as another police vehicle dropped in behind them. Oncoming cars swerved out of the way as the four vehicles slalomed through traffic.

Martin looked around, trying to keep track of the pursuers behind them, as Jack struggled to keep the Chrysler ahead of the more powerful police cars. The one directly behind them accelerated and slammed into the ass-end of the Chrysler. But the pit maneuver didn't work as Jack accelerated away.

"You alright?" Martin called out so he could be heard over the sirens. "Keep your cool, Jack."

Another officer shouted into his mic, "Box him in!"

Sirens blared as a couple more police cars skidded to a stop directly in front of them.

Jack considered his options. The three police vehicles behind were all over him as he wrenched the wheel and swerved, skidding sideways into another street, barely able to maintain control.

The Chrysler sliced through another intersection when an additional cruiser suddenly appeared from a side street and plowed into the front end of the first police car drafting Jack. The impact spun it around into the path of the two trailing police vehicles, which were destroyed by the violent collision - triggering car alarms and airbags - completely blocking the intersection with crumpled metal, smoke, steam, and dying sirens.

Jack glanced up at the rearview. "I think we lost them."

"How you doin', Jack?" Martin questioned like he really cared.

"That's thoughtful of you," Jack said.

"That wasn't so hard." Martin smiled to himself and started to laugh under his breath.

"What's so fucking funny?" Jack asked as the Chrysler roared out of Truth or Consequences.

CHAPTER 6

"Suspects are believed to be traveling north on Interstate 25. Pursuit is NOT terminated. Repeat, not terminated."

Shred looked at R.T. and said, "Suspects?"

R.T. looked up from a picture of Jack on his laptop. "I found something on Mathews, if that's his real name. Check it out."

They both sat in silence as they watched the screen - a NASCAR race was being replayed: earsplitting thunder, then dozens of stock cars exploded into the frame and roared by in a blur. Another angle showed them roaring along smoothly in a pack only inches from each other, trying to break the draft.

"That's him in 18," R.T. said.

In the video, Jack moved up on the car in front of him and broke out of the draft. Then he moved up rapidly and moved outside, running nose to nose with the leader. The two cars were glued together going into the turn, side by side, running wheel to wheel. Jack geared down, stomped on the gas, and went sideways. All four tires smoked and then went backward, which sent him airborne. He helicoptered into the air, crashed down, and burst into flames, going end over end.

R.T. froze the image of the fiery crash and looked up at Shred. "That's all I got. Nothing after the crash. He never raced again." He tapped on the keys of his laptop and went to another site. "It's crazy; the driver's name is Rooster Johnson. I found this picture of Rooster Johnson on Facebook, but I can't find anything else on Mathews. It's like he doesn't exist."

Then he pulled up a split screen of Rooster Johnson and Jack

Mathews. They appeared to be one and the same.

Shred looked up. "Until now."

***

Sam walked in and let the restroom door slam shut behind her. She briefly looked around. It was a tiny room with a small mesh-covered window. She paced in a circle, finally stopped and grabbed the sink, and stared at her reflection in the mirror.

She took a deep breath, leaned in closer, and muttered under her breath, "Goddammit, Jack… goddammit." Then she walked back, looked through the small window, and checked outside. The man sat in the pick-up in the parking lot of the gas station. Waiting. He slowly turned toward the building, almost as if he was staring at her. She jerked her head back, away from the window.

Sam leaned against the sink, her breathing controlled as she reached down into her backpack and pulled out a 9mm Glock. She held it up and checked to make sure it had a round in the chamber. After a beat, Sam stuck it back into the backpack and looked down for a moment. She looked around, trying to think. She closed her eyes, took a deep breath, and then exited the restroom.

The man checked his watch as she walked out of the building. He glanced at her, thinking.

He started the engine as Sam slid into the passenger seat. The look in his eyes indicated that he thought there was something wrong, though he couldn't quite put his finger on it. "What's the matter?" he asked.

Sam shook her head, indicating 'nothing,' as he peeled out of the parking lot.

He looked at her again. "So, for old times sake, I'm gonna tell you something," he said as he eased the pick-up back onto the highway and melded into the flow of traffic. "You should have walked away."

"Yeah? Well, I couldn't," she answered.

"I didn't think so." After a couple of beats, the man continued: "You know, he figured you weren't going to do it. Ahh, the hell with it, life is too short." He looked at Sam again, waiting to see if there was any reaction. There wasn't. Only silence as she stared out the side window.

***

With precision, Jack continued to pass the slower traffic. "It's over. We can't stay on the Interstate," he said as he glanced over at Martin. "We've got to dump this car; this was a pretty stupid idea." He noticed Martin staring at him as if he were an exotic bug.

"Yet here we sit," Martin said as he continued to stare at him.

Jack glanced at Martin again. "What? What are you looking at?"

Martin shook his head, indicating 'nothing,' then he cocked his head as if reappraising Jack. With a smile, he questioned, "Why don't we cut the chit-chat. Get to what's on your mind."

"What do you know about me?" Jack asked in a suddenly direct manner.

"Everything. But I really wanted to see who you were, Jack."

"What?" Jack responded. Martin just sat there and continued to watch him. "It doesn't matter who I am," Jack said. "Who I am means absolutely nothing." Then he gave Martin a 'who the fuck are you?' look. "Huh, Who are you?"

The question had many answers. Finally, Martin said, "A civilized man." He leaned in closer and continued quietly, "Something else you need to say to me? You expect me to believe you don't know who I am. Do you?" He smiled to himself. "I exist in a world beyond your world. One that you could only fantasize about."

"What a bunch of horseshit. It sounds like some bullshit movie line," Jack said under his breath.

Martin continued, "Kinda heady, intoxicating… most people can't comprehend it." He laughed to himself. "It's almost surreal. Quite simple, really. You see, I take what I want, then I leave."

"Why are you telling me this. Do I give a shit? No," Jack said.

Martin smiled, then looked at Jack again. "Relax, Jack. C'mon, you can do better than that."

***

The blazing sun was lower, and the desert mesas' shadows were longer, but the heat was still intense. They were both silent as the Chrysler closed in on an eighteen-wheeler.

As Jack pulled out to pass, he squinted at the road ahead of the semi, and he shot a concerned glance at Martin. In the distance, flashing lights were closing fast. Jack dropped back in behind the semi.

Seconds later, a cruiser screamed by, going in the opposite direction - lights flashing, siren wailing.

Jack looked in the side mirror, then up at the rearview - brake lights. The cruiser locked up as it made a 180-degree turn. Jack pinned the gas, opened the Chrysler up at full throttle, and passed the semi. His eyes flicked up at the rearview again as the cruiser continued to close. "We can't outrun it."

Both vehicles rocketed up the highway, ripping past slower cars as they dodged in and around them - a high-speed slalom run through the slower traffic.

Jack felt like he was inside a video game. He swerved around a slower moving car, and Martin shouted, "Look out!" as a horn blared. Jack whipped back into his lane, inches from getting clipped by the oncoming vehicle.

The Chrysler slewed around the back end of another eighteen-wheeler and went sideways until Jack accelerated and straightened out. Horns blared again as he ducked back in front of the semi.

The cruiser tried the same move but started to swap ends and clipped another oncoming vehicle. It swerved wildly as it rocketed out of control, directly into the path of the semi, which slammed into it, sending it pin-wheeling off the highway as it disappeared in a massive cloud of dust.

***

As the pick-up navigated the traffic on Highway 40, Shred continued his radio tirade: "Well, I see by the smilin' face of my cracked Jimmy Carter watch that it's two o'clock. There's only one thing worse than this Mathew's guy, and that's that he can't be stopped. Well, what a surprise. He's driving a Chrysler 300S Hemi; this beast grunts out 470 horsepower! News flash! He's winning."

Sam looked around as police sirens continued to grow louder behind them. The man checked the rearview mirror: two cruisers were moving in and out of traffic, closing fast behind them. Seconds later, they both streamed by, sirens blaring, and were quickly swallowed up by the traffic heading for Gallup. The man leaned forward, shut off the radio, and took out his cell phone.

***

Martin held his cell phone to his ear as they continued down the flat, empty highway - no civilization in sight. He listened, and after a couple of seconds, he said, "Yeah, I know. Uh-huh, pretty impressive."

Jack glanced at the fuel gauge - less than a quarter tank - then at Martin, who watched him.

"I'll let him know," Martin said as he hung up.

Jack waited for him to say something else. Nothing.

The Chrysler pulled off the highway into the parking lot of a little café-gas station, similar to what you would find on most any open road.

It was empty inside the café, except for a waitress standing behind the counter watching a flickering television. The coverage of Truth or Consequences was all over the news.

It was hot; a slow-moving fan blew the humid air around the café. As she swatted a fly with a fly swatter, she noticed the Chrysler roll to a stop between the gas pumps out front.

Jack and Martin got out. Jack looked back at the empty highway then back at the vacant parking lot. He noticed an old man sitting on the front porch in a wheelchair in the shade. The old man watched them through one milky eye.

Jack warily looked around as he began to pump the gas. He looked up at the old man, then at the café - shapes were barely visible, moving behind the windows, watching them.

Jack spoke softly, "I think it's time to go."

"What?" Martin asked.

"I said, 'I think it's time to go!'" Jack didn't wait for an answer.

Martin suddenly realized what Jack was looking at as the cook burst through the café's door and pumped a round into his shotgun.

The Chrysler's engine roared to life as Martin landed in the passenger seat. Jack lit the Chrysler up, and he looked back at the cook who was going for the kill. The gunshot cracked like thunder, shattering the rear window.

Martin crouched lower as the Chrysler laid rubber through the lot and whipped around the pumps, screeching back onto the highway.

"Motherfucker," Jack said to himself.

Martin looked back as he slowly sat up. "Trigger happy son of a bitch."

Both men remained silent for a couple of seconds. Finally, Jack said, "We're running out of time."

CHAPTER 7

The clock on the wall at the radio station read 2:15. Shred was glued to the TV as the newscast continued:

"Although the full impact of Martin's legacy is still reverberating around the world, it invokes memories of Bernard Madoff's Ponzi scheme - until Martin's, it was the largest in history."

The police scanner was going crazy at the same time; it sounded like a war zone. "Attention, all units. Suspect vehicle is believed to be headed westbound on 52. All units in the area assist code 3."

***

Jack's eyes were locked on the road ahead. The only sound was the droning of the engine and the howling wind as they streaked down Highway 52, converging on a sea of flashing lights. He punched the gas as he headed straight for them.

Martin gave him a concerned glance. "What are you doing?"

A roadblock was forming. Jack continued to accelerate straight at the cruisers - 70…80 mph.

Martin started to freak out and shouted, "What the fuck are you doing?!"

Jack smiled to himself. "Don't worry. It'll be over soon," he answered. Then Jack stomped the parking brake. In a cloud of smoking, burning rubber, the Chrysler spun a screeching 180-degrees. Jack slammed it into reverse and dropped the hammer.

The Chrysler punched through the roadblock, backward. Two of the cruisers were blown cleanly out of the way, spinning off the highway.

Jack spun the Chrysler back around, slammed it into drive, and punched the gas, accelerating to speed as a third cruiser locked up and skidded right past them.

Jack checked the rearview, watched the cruiser, and just shook his head.

Martin shouted, "What the hell was that?"

Jack said nothing.

***

The man and Sam watched the road ahead as traffic was diverted onto Highway 36, two lanes into one. The man rechecked his watch. One hand guided the steering wheel as he turned off onto a narrow dirt road.

Sam gave him a questioning look.

He glanced at her sitting apprehensively at his side and said, "Relax." Then he returned his eyes to the road and accelerated.

***

The Chrysler materialized through the heat waves. After a couple of seconds, flashing lights appeared behind it. Jack gazed up at the mirror. The third cruiser was getting closer, closing the gap. The siren continued to grow louder as he looked ahead at the light traffic.

Suddenly, the Chrysler was hit from behind. Jack fired a look up at the rearview, which was filled with the cruiser as it closed in again. It continued to accelerate and slammed into them a second time. Their heads snapped back. The Chrysler went sideways; Jack nearly lost it, but he regained control as he fired another look up at the mirror.

The police car backed off as they caught up to the slower moving traffic, maintaining less than a car length.

Jack swerved around the first vehicle into oncoming traffic, his eyes locked on an approaching bus. A horn blared as he ducked back in and rechecked the rearview. The cruiser had mirrored his move and was still on his ass. The guy was good.

The cruiser accelerated again and roared up into view alongside the Chrysler. Jack jerked the wheel and slammed into it. The cruiser left the road in a cloud of dust. The trooper quickly recovered and bounced back onto the road - not even fazed as he dropped in directly behind the Chrysler again. The trooper accelerated. A split second later, the cruiser slammed into them like a freight train, and the Chrysler went sideways - spinning out of control. The rear end came off the ground and rotated over, flipping into a violent roll, cartwheeling, spewing glass, and finally coming down hard.

The trooper hung onto his steering wheel. The desert and the highway were a blur as he slammed into the Chrysler again and punched it further down the highway. When everything stopped, the wrecked Chrysler was sitting upside down in the middle of the road - it's motor no longer running.

The police car sat about twenty yards away from the wreck. The trooper was alive. He leaned back in his seat and took a deep breath, then squinted through the windshield at the Chrysler as smoke continued to bellow into the sky. He undid his seatbelt and climbed out, drawing his Glock as he slowly approached the demolished car.

As he got closer, he crouched down and looked inside. The Chrysler was empty.

Behind him, Jack and Martin materialized out of the smoke. Both looked like they'd been through hell. The trooper froze.

Seconds later, the cruiser's engine turned over with a blast of horsepower and roared to life. Jack threw it into gear and gently gave it some gas. The police car rolled down the highway, past the wrecked Chrysler and the unconscious trooper. Back in business.

Both their faces were cut and bruised. Martin just glared at Jack.

Jack glanced over, rubbed his neck, and said, "C'mon, it's not as bad as it looks." Then he looked at the clock on the dash; it was 2:25. His eyes went back to Martin, who was still glaring at him. "I'm aware of the time, Martin."

***

"Suspect vehicle has just T.A.'d with my unit and two other units on 52. Requesting emergency assistance."

The dispatcher's voice cut in, "Roadblocks are being set up east of Quemando and outside Gallup. Suspects are now believed to be headed north on 36 in a state cruiser."

R.T. glanced at Shred. "It doesn't make any sense. They're entering the Zuni Pueblo. It's a sovereign nation. The Zuni have jurisdictional power over everything that happens in their territory. What are they doing on the reservation?"

"Jesus, how the hell would I know?" Shred said. "You tell me, you're the Indian."

R.T. just shook his head, "If it's left up to the tribal police, Martin may disappear for good."

***

A half-hour later, under the blistering sun, heat shimmered around an image trailing a huge plume of dust. The dust began to take form around the approaching cruiser.

Jack and Martin remained quiet as the cruiser ate up the dirt road thirty miles south of Gallup. Jack looked intense and studied the vast expanse of empty land around them. A couple of miles later, they passed through a scattered community littered with wrecked cars on blocks and overpopulated with hungry dogs.

Martin glanced down at his cell phone and moved a cursor across a map of New Mexico to a Pueblo just outside Gallup; then, he double-clicked. A tighter aerial view of an airstrip came up on the screen. It was little more than a dirt road surrounded by a couple of double-wide trailers. He looked relieved; it felt like he was home free.

***

The pickup flew down the dirt road, throwing up red dust and gravel. A bent metal sign covered with rusted bullet holes became visible when the dust cleared. It read: "Entering Zuni Indian Reservation Lands."

Three old Indians sat motionless on the front porch of a flat-roofed reservation bar. Their eyes followed the pickup as it passed and disappeared down the dirt road.

***

An ancient Airstream trailer sat half swallowed up by weeds and sported a small satellite dish on the roof. Chickens scratched around in the dirt. A couple of stripped junk cars sat up on blocks in the overgrown yard.

The buzzing of horseflies was the only sound in the eerie silence.

An old Indian leaned against the trailer. He pulled out an unfiltered cigarette and lit up like it was a perfect science. He thought he heard something, then dismissed it as he looked around. His gaze shifted to the empty dirt airstrip. Nothing. He looked in the other direction at the distant mesas. Nothing. Then he looked up, squinting into the sun.

Suddenly, the sound of an approaching vehicle interrupted the stillness. A chained, scruffy looking Rottweiler snapped to attention, growling low.

The old Indian exhaled and walked around the side of the trailer. He stopped next to a dilapidated outhouse and watched the cruiser as it approached, followed by a huge plume of dust. His dark eyes followed it for several moments, then focused back on his cigarette.

***

The cruiser flew down the dirt road past a couple of double-wide trailers. The old Airstream was visible in the distance. A few minutes later, it rolled to a stop in front of it.

Jack cut the engine and looked out at the empty airstrip. Dust blew in from the surrounding desert. The digital clock on the dash switched to three o'clock.

Both men climbed out and stood on opposite sides of the police car. "Where's Sam?" Jack asked as he warily looked past Martin. A feeling caught Jack's sixth sense, and he knew he was being watched.

Martin gave a half-laugh, then softly and strangely muttered, "Soon. She'll be here soon."

Jack focused on an old beat-up pickup truck next to the trailer. The truck had no hood. The old Indian leaned over the fender, pouring oil from a can into a funnel. His eyes never left them.

The trailer door opened a crack. A dark, weather-beaten face was barely visible. An Indian woman pushed open the screen door and motioned with her hand for the old Indian to come back inside. Then she yelled something Jack didn't understand and disappeared into the trailer.

"Get it through your head. No one is coming to save the day," Martin said. "The bad guy gets away at the end of this story."

"What makes you think you're going to get away with anything?" Jack replied.

Martin looked out at the pickup as it approached. "I already have."

The pickup barreled down the dirt road toward the airstrip. The man glanced at Sam and said, "You ready?"

Sam nodded as she continued to stare straight ahead at Jack and Martin.

Jack watched the pickup approach. It didn't stop until it was close enough that Jack could see Sam's face through the windshield. The truck rolled to a stop directly behind the cruiser. The man remained calm as he checked the rearview; the road was empty behind them.

Sam took a deep breath, grabbed her backpack, and climbed out. She and the man stopped short of Jack and Martin. Sam and Jack looked at each other for a moment. Jack thought she looked slightly embarrassed.

Martin threw a quick look at the old Indian. Then the Indian disappeared inside the trailer, letting the screen door slap shut behind him.

Sam just silently stood there - one eye on Jack, one eye on Martin.

Jack smiled halfway at her, then nodded at the man. "Who's this? What's going on? Sam?"

Martin answered, "My wife's been with my brother."

"Your wife?" Jack flatly said. He looked back at Sam, and their eyes met. For a moment, Jack's face went dead cold as he stared at her.

"Yeah, my wife," Martin said.

A silent moment revealed the confusion on Jack's face. "What are you talking about?"

"Relax," Martin said. "Like I told you, I know everything there is to know about you, Jack."

Jack looked at Sam, then back at Martin. "Is this some kind of joke?"

"Afraid not," Martin said. "Let's just cut through the pleasantries and bullshit, huh?"

"Fuck you," Jack snapped.

The Indian woman inside the trailer flipped through the channels on the TV. She stopped on the news and watched the cell phone footage two good samaritans recorded earlier in Truth or Consequences – the incident had to be the biggest thing to hit town in a long time.

The old Indian stood at the window with one eye on Martin and Jack, the other on the TV as he watched the Chrysler flash by, followed by the police cruisers.

CHAPTER 8

"Freeze it!" Shred said, his eyes focused on the frozen silhouette of the passenger in the Chrysler. "Who's this guy?"

R.T.'s eyes never left his computer as he answered, "That's him. Daniel Martin. Talk about a strong sense of entitlement. People rob banks because that's where the money is. This guy is a monster, stealing billions from innocent people – mostly pension plans and charitable foundations." He glanced at Shred. "Destroying whole lives ... he made billions without pulling a gun."

Shred continued to stare at the screen as R.T. pulled up the image of Sam. He looked up at R.T. "The fish stinks from the head down. There's no way she couldn't have known."

R.T looked at Shred. "If these guys are using a cell, it's gotta have a GPS. They should be able to track them unless they're using burners."

The scanner came alive again with police chatter: "All units, be advised tribal police will exercise criminal jurisdiction over any activities on the Zuni Pueblo."

***

Martin didn't even look up at the sound of the old Indian's footsteps as he walked up and handed him a briefcase.

Eyeing Sam, the old Indian nodded to Martin, then uneasily stared at Jack. He cautiously looked between the two, then shot his hawk-black eyes to Martin. He spoke just above a whisper in Shiwi', a Zuni dialect. When he finished, he turned a questioning look at

Jack, who didn't flinch.

Martin nodded slowly, then seriously looked at the Indian and said, "Thank you." Then he gave a nod to his brother, who put his hand on the Indian's shoulder and walked him back to the trailer.

Martin's eyes flicked back at Jack. "He's unhappy with you because he said he knows you. He says he saw you in a vision. Crazy shit, huh?" he smiled and glanced up at the faint distant whine of an engine.

Jack heard it too. His gaze followed Martin's as a single engine Cessna suddenly crested the hill directly above them.

"Next stop, Canada," Martin said as he smiled to himself, his eyes transfixed on the plane. "Time for a little tune-up. I've changed my identity so many times; I don't even know what I look like anymore." After a beat, he said, "So here we are."

Sweating in the hot sun, Martin started around the cruiser. "Do you really think I wanted it to come to this? Do you Jack? I don't particularly like killing, but I want you to know that this is one I'm going to enjoy." He continued past him toward Sam. "Not sure what she saw in you anyway."

Jack started to say something but hesitated; he'd felt the presence of Martin's brother as he stepped up behind him.

Martin stopped dead. He stared at Sam and the 9mm that dangled by her side. His grin faded as he rubbed his neck, trying to figure out what he was missing. "Terrific," he said. "Now I guess I'm a little slow here. Samantha?"

A silent moment hung between them. Watching everyone, Sam's eyes smoothly moved from side to side as he continued. "What exactly are you doing?" An unsure silence lingered. "Things'er okay?"

Sam leveled a serious look at him and said, "I'm doing this because of you."

"Because of me?" he asked.

"You said you were going to let him live if I did what you said."

Martin suddenly lost his attitude, his manner devoid of its usual cockiness. Finally, he said, "So, it's like this, is it?" With a menacing stare, he hesitantly replied, "I'm not sure where this fits into the game plan, sweetheart."

Martin and his brother traded a serious stare.

Sam's eyes were stone cold. "Oh, it doesn't," she said.

"Really. What makes you so different than me?" Martin asked, his tone incredulous. "You go ahead. Shoot me if you want, Samantha. But you'll be dead before you hit the ground."

Jack glanced up at the plane as it passed overhead.

Martin nodded at his brother. Without warning, his brother spun and pulled a .40 caliber - the move so fast, it was performed with the grace of a professional killer.

Sam fired once, and the shot racked him like a bolt of lightning - the impact blew his sunglasses straight up in the air as it carried him backward.

The old Indian peeked out the window as the second shot blew him cleanly away. The two shots echoed across the desert. The Rottweiler began to bark like crazy.

"What just happened?" Martin raised his hands and quietly said, "Ah… Jesus." He glanced down at his brother. "Seems I was wrong." Then he held his arms out, making it clear he wasn't going for his gun. Martin raised his hands higher and took a small step back.

Jack glanced at Sam. She took a deep breath and reassembled her composure. "It's not your fault," Jack said. "It was the only way out."

Martin took another step back. "Maybe we need to rethink this."

"Wishful thinking," Sam answered. Their eyes met an instant before she squeezed the trigger. The bullet punched her husband in the chest, and he was driven straight back to the ground.

Flat on his back, Martin's eyes blinked open. He sucked air through his teeth and stared straight up at the empty sky, trying to focus. His brother was also flat on his back a few feet away, and he wasn't breathing.

Sam slowly stepped into view, directly over him.

Silent, Martin stared up at Sam as Jack stepped in alongside her. In shock, he coughed up bloody spittle and choked out, "Aren't you going to say anything?"

"You got a cell phone; call an ambulance," Jack said.

"Congratulations, you win, asshole," Martin whispered. "You almost had me. Maybe next time."

Sam looked at Jack. "What's he talking about?"

Barely audible, Martin whispered, "I know who he is," then died.

She glanced up at Jack. "What was he talking about?"

Jack didn't answer; the only sound was the mournful howling of the wind.

Both appeared shocked by her actions, but Sam made it a point to look into his eyes. "Who are you? What's going on, Jack?"

Jack watched her with complete indifference and stared square into her sunglasses. Finally, he said, "I can't see your eyes."

She slipped off the sunglasses. "It's been two years; I hadn't heard a word. Nothing. Then his brother called and said he'd kill you if I didn't do what he said." After a couple of beats, she sighed, "It was over; Martin and I were over."

"Except it never is really quite over," Jack said.

The old Indian rummaged around the trailer, trying to find what he wanted. The old woman sat like a gargoyle in the corner, weeping. He finally found what he was looking for and pulled out a cell phone, circa the 1990s. Then he moved back to the window and dialed. He leaned against the wall as he watched Jack and Sam, waiting.

"I had no idea what he was doing," Sam said. "He shut me out. It was all one big lie. In some ways, I understand him doing it. I didn't have to like it, but I understood it. But you?"

Jack stared at her. Something like panic flickered in her eyes, then she matter-of-factly said, "You've been planning this for months, haven't you?"

"Are you alright?" he asked.

"I always told myself I wasn't going to end up like this." Staring at him, she lamented, "And now here I am. What the fuck am I doing? Am I alright?" Jack remained silent. "What do you think? I just killed my husband. I'm just fucking great." After a beat, she whispered, "I thought you loved me. Who are you, Jack?"

"This isn't about me," he said. "It's about the job I had to do."

"And what job is that?" she asked.

"I'm a thief," he quietly said as he slowly walked over and picked up the briefcase.

"How the hell was this going to work?" she asked. "Based on what fairy tale? You knew that, didn't you?"

Jack looked away as Sam restrained herself and quietly demanded, "Say something, goddammit. I want the truth."

He glanced down at Martin's body. "They were setting up his extradition when you asked me to go to Mexico."

"I'm not an idiot," she snapped. "I see what you're doing." She looked down at the briefcase. "What's inside?"

He hesitated, then said, "I'm not sure you want to know.

"Who are you working for, Jack?"

"A private party. Does it matter?"

"What are they paying you, Jack? A piece of the action?"

He glanced up at the plane as it looped back. "It's complicated."

"It always is," she said.

CHAPTER 9

A couple of years after Jack retired from the racing circuit, a friend from school, by the name of Stephen Wills, contacted him.

Wills was a trader at The DeBeers Group. They had offices in New York, Luxembourg, South Africa, and Canada. The company dealt primarily with Rough Diamonds. Also known as Impact Diamonds, the raw gems were ideal for industrial and scientific use.

As he explained to Jack, Wills had completed fifty-six transactions for his employer worth six billion dollars in diamonds over the previous year. And Wills was done; it was time to get out.

So when they met, Wills shared that his portfolio had accumulated over forty million dollars worth of Rough Diamonds during his time at The DeBeers Group. It was time for his last transaction. Wills vetted a list of prospective buyers and narrowed it down to one: Daniel Martin.

Although Wills knew who and what Martin was, it didn't matter. It was set to be the biggest transaction of his life.

The problem was Wills needed someone to get close to Martin's estranged wife, Samantha. That's where Jack came in – Wills needed to know everything there was to know about Daniel Martin. And Jack would be paid a million dollars for the information.

The problem was Martin had been arrested in Mexico. So, the first step was to get Martin out before he could be extradited to the United States. Wills knew Mexican officials could be bought, but that wasn't the issue.

A plan formed: when Martin's escape was arranged and Martin was out, the money would be wired into Wills' personal account.

After which, the diamonds would be given to Martin's brother.

Martin and his brother came up with an idea to get him back into the United States, where his brother would have the diamonds waiting for him in Gallup.

***

A week after the deal was made, a black Chrysler 300S sat under fluorescent lights on a lift in the middle of a facility in Albuquerque, New Mexico.

The room was a beehive of activity. Sparks flying, one man worked on an angle grinder, and another welded roll tubing. A second group of men raked the entire suspension. The engine was getting tweaked - a mechanic revved the motor, testing and listening.

Martin's brother handed a man an envelope. They watched another man study a diagram of the rig to be built into the trunk of the Chrysler.

All they needed was a driver.

What they didn't take into account was that Jack had also done his homework. He knew everything there was to know about Martin and his family. When he saw Sam's exchange with Martin's brother in the bar in Casa Grandes, he knew it was game on.

CHAPTER 10

Jack glanced back at the low flying Cessna as it made it's final approach, then at Sam.

"What about you, Jack?"

"What about me?" he asked.

Matching his intensity, she said, "I kept you alive."

Unflinching, Jack stared at her.

"I saved your life," she repeated.

He looked away as the plane touched down. "You shouldn't have."

She laughed bitterly and said, "I guess you were right about me. Funny how we really don't take the time to reflect on things we think we know … how it's going to end."

Jack studied her for a moment. He'd caught the faintest hint of regret in her voice as she continued, "Everything doesn't always end the way you think it will."

Jack remained silent. He looked over at the trailer. "I'm not the only loose end here."

"What are you talking about?" She followed his eyes to the old Indian who peeked out the window watching them.

"The Zuni have a strict honor code. When someone saves another's life, they're indebted to them forever. Blood Brothers," he said.

"What?" she asked, her voice rising. "What does that have to do with me?"

"That man in there was in Vietnam with Daniel's father, who saved his life. Martin's brother was here last week. Safeguarding this briefcase was a debt of gratitude."

Sam's eyes flicked back to Jack with a little more urgency now. "I'm going to get on that plane," she said. "You're never going to see me again."

In the distance, the wail of sirens grew louder.

She squinted at the cloud of dust rising on the horizon, then turned back, perfectly at ease, with her 9mm leveled at Jack, who was waiting with his 9mm leveled at her.

Sam never lost eye contact with him, and for a moment, he sensed her attitude could go either way - outrage or some sense of being flattered. She chose the latter and said, "Game on, huh?"

After a tense beat, neither was sure how the situation would go. Dumbfounded, Sam stared at Jack. A moment passed between them, and she shook her head. Her eyes bored into him, and finally she asked, "What are you doing? You have a gun. Why would you have a gun?" Her words hung in the air, but Jack didn't respond.

Her look was difficult to read. Time froze. "What do you want?" she asked.

"Everything," he said.

"You're starting to sound like him." Their eyes bore into each other's, and Sam glanced down at the briefcase, realization setting in. "Who are you, Jack?"

"That's not my name."

"Who the hell are you?" she snapped.

"It's a little hard to explain."

Her eyes flashed as she said, "Try." She thought about it for a couple of seconds and mumbled, "I think I'm starting to figure it out."

"Better late than never," he said.

In an instant of blind clarity, she knew. Her eyes flooded, and the gun trembled. Tears dripped down her cheeks. "You used me."

Jack remained silent as the Cessna taxied toward them.

Angry and tearful, she asked, "Is it easier now? Not pretending?" Despite the tears, her eyes were ice cold. "I'd like to know something, Jack. It probably doesn't matter in the final scheme of things…" Sam paused and looked into his eyes. "Did you ever love me?"

He looked away so quickly it was like saying "yes," she thought.

"Does it matter?" he asked, then softly answered, "Yes."

"Is that the truth? Why in the world should I believe you, Jack?"

"Because I'm telling you the truth," he said. "What about you?"

She stood there a moment. The air went out of her, and she realized he was telling the truth. Then she slowly nodded.

"Is that the truth?" he asked.

"Yes," she answered. "If you pretend to mean it, I'll pretend I believe it." Then softly, Sam said, "Jesus, Jack. I guess we both have what the other one needs."

In that frozen moment, everything was suddenly out in the open. Through tears, Sam put her game face back on. "Leave with me. What do you say?"

"Nah, not my style," he said as he glanced at the approaching vehicles. "Creature of habit, I suppose. I think I'll keep my options open."

"What does that mean?"

Jack shared a smile filled with bittersweet affection.

In a barely audible whisper, she asked, "Why? Why Jack?" Then Sam shook her head and sighed, "God, I hate you."

"Good. I hate you too," he softly replied.

They stood in silence before he finally said, "What got broken here won't go back together."

Jack looked at the vehicles. "What the hell?" He lowered his 9mm. "You better not miss your flight."

She lowered her 9mm, realizing he was letting her go. It was goodbye.

"You gotta go now."

Eyes fixed on each other, they both knew it was the only way this had a happy ending.

"Will I ever see you again?" she asked.

There was no answer. There were no words.

Jack stepped closer; his eyes met hers as he reached up and brushed a strand of hair out of her face. With a slight smile, he said, "Life's messy, isn't it?"

"You know, I'd give up everything for just a little more time," she said. "Did I win, or did we both lose?" There was no answer.

They both smiled as Sam turned away and walked to the plane.

Jack watched her as she made her way up the metal staircase.

Three Zuni Police Department SUVs roared up the dirt road toward him as the plane cleared the runway and lifted off into the sky.

Sam stared out the window at the patrol cars as they arrived. In the swirling dust, she could make out a lone man staring up at the plane.

Jack smiled faintly to himself, then became serious again. He continued to stare after something he would never see again.

A melancholy smile touched Sam's face, emptiness reflected in her eyes before they shut.

Amid the swirling dust, Jack slowly raised his arms as the reservation police climbed out of the vehicles and moved past him to the dead bodies.

The old Indian stood in the doorway of the trailer and stared at the shape in the swirling dust. As it cleared for a second, he saw Jack staring back at him; then, the dust swallowed him up again.

A couple of seconds later, it cleared. Jack and the briefcase were gone.

Somewhere, "Rooster" by Alice in Chains played on.

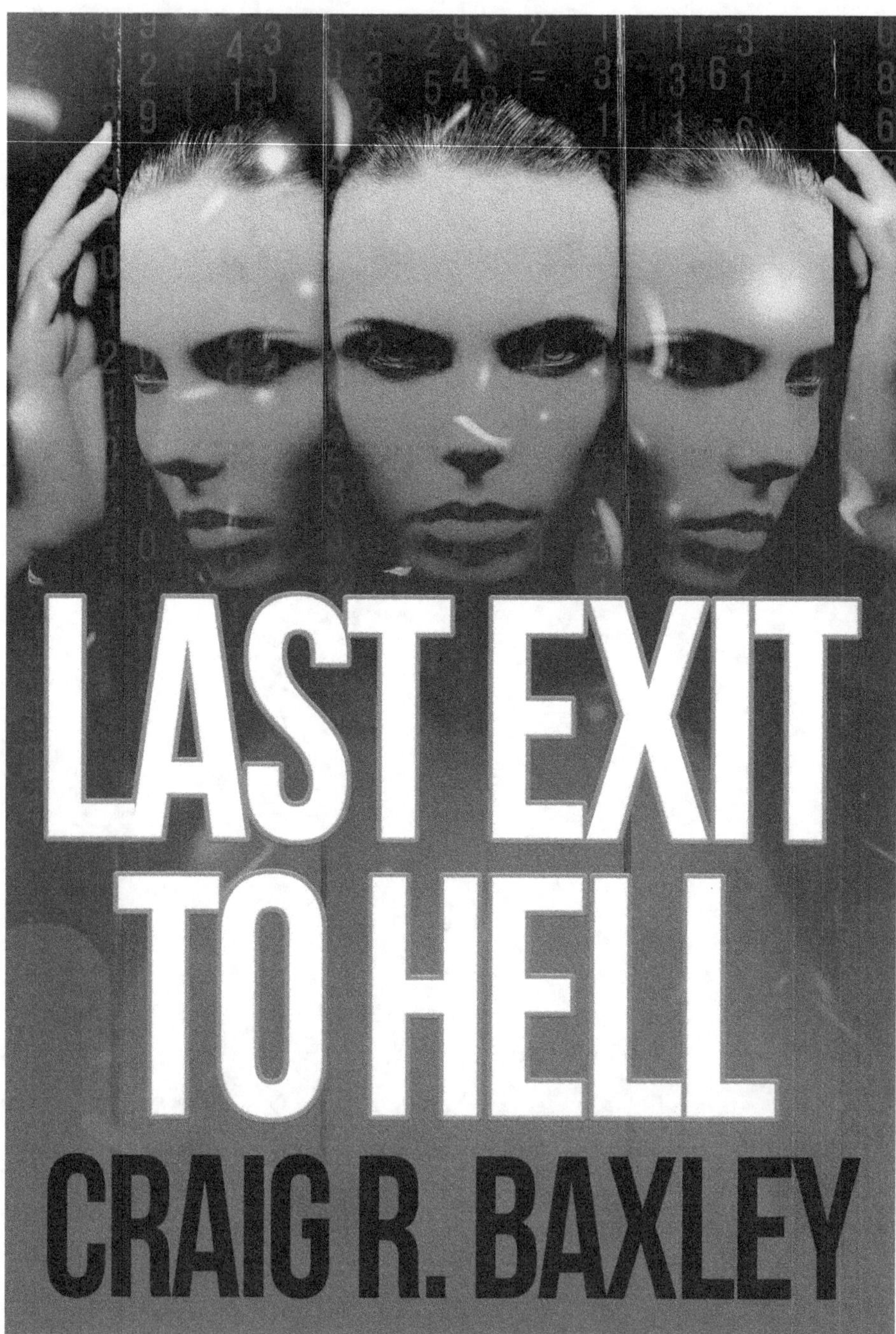

LAST EXIT
TO HELL
CRAIG R. BAXLEY

BOOK PREVIEW

Excerpt from "Last Exit to Hell"

It had been 2,027 days since a massive technological failure brought the entire planet to a standstill. The population became consumed by images of what people thought they wanted to be, never realizing that those images were slowly taking over and assimilating their world.

Nobody could remember the exact moment when they lost control of their lives. But it happened; and, there wasn't anything they could do about it.

Man's entire existence had been cataloged into bytes of information – every shred of humanity – all passed into a melting pot of deleted programs. Glitches. Viruses and updates. It was a wave of information that defined everything about the human race.

Meanwhile, quantum computers explored a parallel universe with shared memory and distributed it with memory virtualization that caused a split. The quantum gateway completed a circuit between reality and the parallel world – a world built on a reflection of people as they truly are: all the good, the bad, the evil, and the ugly. In essence, life became a virtual bridge between heaven and hell.

Those that still knew the truth fought to take back what remained of their world. Borders were overrun. The suffering and loss grew to an epic scale. Then came the Plague. Suddenly there was nothing left, just the few that survived.

Those who remained called themselves Clans, and these ravaged creatures were starving. Cannibalism was a rampant necessity that ensured survival since only human blood could guide them to the portal. The lost souls who had gone to the other side were waiting. Those caught in the between, the "Glitches," were their only hope. Only they could free them. It was their blood that would end their pain.

* * * * *

"Last Exit to Hell"
Coming in 2022
by Craig R. Baxley

ABOUT THE AUTHOR

Craig Baxley is a third-generation filmmaker. After starting his career in front of the camera, Craig worked his way up as a successful stunt coordinator and second unit director on films like *Predator, Reds, The Long Riders,* and *The Warriors* with such talented directors as Don Siegel, Alan Pakula, Warren Beatty, Norman Jewison, Walter Hill, and Steven Spielberg, after which he transitioned – making his directorial debut on the acclaimed hit series, *The A-Team.*

His first feature film, *Action Jackson,* for Joel Silver, was the beginning of a very diverse career working in many genres. Craig later went on to direct a number of mini-series, including Stephen King's *Storm of the Century* and *Rose Red,* along with the entire television series, *Kingdom Hospital.* Craig also directed Bryan Singer's *The Triangle* and *The Lost Room.*

His memoir, *Driven,* is available at retailers worldwide.

Craig and his wife, Valerie, live on the water in Jupiter, Florida.

ACKNOWLEDGMENTS

I would like to thank all my friends in New Mexico for our life experiences together.

My sincere appreciation to my invaluable first readers: Valerie Baxley, Adam Howe, and Al Leong. Thank you.

And once again, it was a pleasure to work with my amazing editor, Michele Dalton.